FRANKIE SPARROW:

Private Investigator

Ewan McGregor

First published in 2018
Copyright © Ewan McGregor
Formatting by Polgarus Studio

Cover images © Shutterstock (Birds)
Cover by Stuart Bache www.bookscovered.co.uk

For Tricia and Aaron

To be kept informed of any new releases and to receive some exclusive freebies, sign up for The Frankie Sparrow Newsletter. Details can be found at the end of this book.

CHAPTER 1

Trouble for Frankie Sparrow

Frankie Sparrow had just finished detention. Mr Finch always gave him detention. He hadn't even done anything wrong.

Well, that wasn't strictly true, but Mr Finch had over-reacted, as usual.

Frankie didn't hang about; he flew from school as soon as the bell sounded, leaving all thoughts of detention, homework and unreasonable teacher's behind. It was the start of the school holidays and he now had two whole months to do as he pleased.

Because of Mr Finch, Frankie was an hour late meeting his friends.

"We thought you were going to miss all the fun!" Kal said.

Frankie, Kal, Geego and Spark, always met in their clubhouse which they had built in a large tree overlooking a row of human houses. They called it 'The Den'.

From The Den, the four young sparrows could scope out potential targets, unsuspecting victims of their favourite and most risky game; "Keek-a-boo". The game involved aiming their droppings at the human's who walked below. It was disgusting but the young sparrows loved it. They didn't even care that it was illegal - the Pigeon Police had quite rightly banned the game years ago.

The sparrows scanned the ground below.

"Here comes one now!" Kal cried, after a few minutes of searching. All four friends moved into position, buzzing with excitement.

Beneath them, a man emerged from his house and awkwardly locked the door. *Awkwardly,* because he carried in his arms an array of items: - a huge briefcase in one hand; a large flask in the other; an umbrella tucked under his left arm; a bulky winter coat slung over the right. Car keys dangled from his mouth. The young sparrows could see the man was headed for his car, which was perfectly positioned under their tree.

"Wait until he's right below us and opens his door ..." Frankie whispered.

The man fumbled with his keys, aimed them at his brand new shiny black car and moved in to open the door.

Little did he know that, above him, the sparrows were poised …

"Go, go, go!!" shouted Geego and Spark in unison.

Splat! Splat!! *SPLAT!!!*

The dropping's came from all directions.

"Direct hit!"

The man was helpless against the torrent of bird droppings raining down. His belongings were thrown high into the air and both he and his car were covered in a stinking white and yellow goo. The man shouted angrily at the tree above, gathered up his soiled possessions and moved to return to the house. The new car now resembled a Dalmatian. The sparrows couldn't contain their laughter.

"That was the best one yet!" giggled Frankie.

However, he was the only one still laughing …

His three friends had stopped suddenly; their eyes raised upwards,

They stared at the angry sparrow hovering behind him.

"Frankie!!!"

Uh oh.

The three other sparrows had spotted Frankie's father flying over to them. They were frozen to the spot. Frankie's dad, Harry, was a sparrow that wouldn't stand for any bad behaviour. He had caught them red handed.

"What have I told you about this disgusting game? No wonder we birds get a bad name with this nonsense going on." All four young sparrows looked sheepishly downwards.

"Think yourselves lucky I'm in a good mood but if I ever hear about any of you playing this game again, I'll be informing your parents before you can say Percy Pigeon! Get back to your nests **NOW!!**"

The young sparrows didn't need to be told twice. They flew away, leaving Frankie to face the music.

"How many times do I need to tell you about playing this silly game, Frankie?" his father growled. "What are we going to do with you? I know it's the school holidays but you're grounded. No, better still …- I think you need to get a job!"

"A job? But …" Frankie was tongue tied.

"It's sorted. You're coming to work with me!"

CHAPTER 2
The Pigeon Detectives

Detective Doolan was not happy. As the leader of the Pigeon Detectives he was responsible for keeping crime low. In recent weeks, however, there had been a spate of nest robberies. Worst of all, the victims of these robberies were all Very Important Birds.

It was the last thing he needed, with elections for Pigeon Detective leader taking place soon. There was no way he would be re-elected if the robberies continued, especially as it was the Parliament of Owls who were being targeted, (the same owls who made the all-important decisions).

Detective Doolan had a meeting scheduled, later in the week, with Peggy Beans, the head of the Parliament. How was he going to tell her that no progress had been made? It was embarrassing. So, when Doolan entered the Pigeon Police nest, to see his squad of detectives huddled around a newspaper, *laughing*, he was furious.

Doolan flew quickly over to his team: "Something funny here?" he enquired.

The five pigeons adjusted themselves to their boss's arrival. Not one of them had a response to the question.

"No, I didn't think so." Doolan answered for them.

"That's five nests broken into now, so we don't have time to sit around laughing and reading newspapers. We need to find out who is doing this. Get to work!"

The detectives made their way to the exit. The only one who remained was a large pigeon. He hadn't been part of the main group. Instead he sat at a table on his own.

"Can I have a word, Boss?" the pigeon asked.

"What is it, Detective Pratchett?"

Detective Paulie Pratchett was enormous, and liked to wear a large flat cap. He thought it made him look smart. It didn't.

"I've been talking to a few of my contacts and I reckon I'm ready to bring in the nest robber. The rest of these birds couldn't catch a worm never mind a criminal." Pratchett rubbed his wing tips together with glee.

"That's great news, but make sure you have the right bird. I don't want you cutting any corners." Doolan looked very sceptical. Everyone knew Pratchett wasn't to be trusted. The large bird had been warned for his behaviour, and methods, before.

"Don't you worry about that - I'll have the nest robber in custody before close of play today." replied Pratchett, smugly, before flying off.

Doolan knew that something didn't add up. What was Pratchett up to?

CHAPTER 3

Wakey, wakey Frankie!

Trouble seemed to follow Frankie Sparrow around. He couldn't help getting into mischief and this time he was paying for it. Usually on school holidays there was nothing he enjoyed more than a nice long lie in his comfy bed but today he had to *work*. It just wasn't fair.

Harry Sparrow crept up the stairs to his son's room. He didn't want to wake his sleeping wife and daughter. He entered the room and saw Frankie sound asleep. It was 4am.

"Frankie…" Harry called, in hushed tones, from the door. There was no response apart from his son's snoring.

He tried again, "Frankie! C'mon, we need to get going."

No answer …

"**FRANKIE!!!!**" Harry shouted from three claws away. This did the trick, the youngster bounced out of his deep sleep and out of bed. Unfortunately, Harry had woken the whole family.

"Wh ... wh ... what's happening? What's going on? Dad?" Frankie didn't know who he *was,* at that moment, never mind what time of day it was.

"I don't want to go to school today!" he mumbled, still half-asleep.

"It's the school holidays, Son, remember? You're coming to work with me. Get yourself ready and be downstairs in two minutes. I've even made you breakfast, so don't say I'm not good to you."

Frankie was still in a sleepy daze but got himself ready as quickly as he could. He stumbled downstairs to where his father was waiting, patiently, in the kitchen. A full sparrow breakfast was laid out on the table: a mixture of worms, nuts, breadcrumbs, seeds, berries, insects and scraps. Delicious. This would set him up for the day.

Harry watched as Frankie started eating his breakfast only to fall fast asleep again in his chair, his beak sliding into the plate full of food.

"Frankie!!" Harry shouted, rousing his son from sleep again.

"I'm up! I'm up!" Frankie spluttered, his eyes still half shut.

"Let's go son, we're late as it is."

One thing was for sure - it was going to be a long day.

CHAPTER 4

Pratchett on the prowl

Detective Pratchett left the Pigeon Police nest in a hurry. He was flying to meet a small robin who had been keeping an eye on a suspect.

Jeff Robin was hungry. He hadn't eaten in days, and was looking forward to the lovely breakfast roll he had just bought from The Bird Stop cafe. He was just about to take his first bite when, out of nowhere, Pratchett swooped down and swiped the roll from his grasp before swallowing it in one huge gulp.

"Where is the suspect?" Pratchett asked the shocked little robin, flecks of bread spraying from his beak.

"In the cafe. He's having a breakfa-"

"Nobody needs to know what he's doing. I can see that for myself. Planning another robbery, no doubt," Pratchett interrupted. He was in no mood to be nice, and he had no time for this little robin. Everyone thought robins seemed like lovely little birds, as far as Pratchett was concerned, they were good-for-nothing pests. He could see the magpie suspect wolfing down his breakfast. *Enjoy your meal. It will be your last as a free bird,* he thought to himself with glee.

"He's not done anything wrong yet," Jeff said gingerly.

"Nothing wrong? That's for me to decide. I can take it from here. You can leave." Pratchett dismissed the little robin.

Just at that moment however, the magpie rose from his table and headed for the exit.

"Don't go just yet! You might be useful for once in your life. I want you to tail this magpie. I'll be following on just behind you. Can you manage that without messing it up?" Pratchett snapped.

The small bird nodded. He knew Pratchett didn't like to do any work if someone else could do it for him. He didn't have a problem taking the credit though. The little robin started to creep behind the large magpie. Pratchett, instead of following on as he said he would, stayed behind in the cafe. He was still hungry.

The magpie moved slowly. He was flying on a full stomach after spending so long in the cafe. Jeff Robin flew cautiously behind him. Suddenly however, the magpie burst into life. He abruptly changed gear and darted away, Jeff was in danger of losing him, Pratchett would *never* have kept up. Jeff flew faster and faster until the magpie was back in his sights.

The magpie must have sensed he was being tailed. He turned and, when he saw that his pursuer was a tiny robin, he stopped, made a quick U-turn, and started flying in the little robin's direction! Jeff quickly put on his brakes, turned on his talons and sped away. The tables had turned. Jeff was now the one being chased! If he was caught there was no telling what the magpie might do to him. Jeff was terrified! He flew quickly but the magpie was unusually fast.

Jeff, however, was a smart and nimble little robin. He flew one way then quickly darted downwards, using his lack of size to his advantage. He took refuge in a low-lying bush.

Jeff's heart beat furiously. He could see the magpie had lost sight of him but was still searching. He froze to the spot whilst the magpie looked high and low.

"Leave me alone! Just leave me alone!" the magpie shouted, in Jeff's general direction before speeding away. Jeff let out a shaking breath, relieved that he had survived, but then realised he had failed his task.

Pratchett would be furious.

CHAPTER 5

Nest-building for novices

All sparrows have jobs. In fact, *most* birds have jobs. Apart from crows. Crows are very lazy. Lazy and untrustworthy. Never, *ever* trust a crow.

Harry Sparrow was a nest builder. He was, probably, the best nest builder around. And, now, Frankie was going to work with him during the school holidays. He wondered what his friends would be up to today, while he was stuck at the building site. No doubt they were still sleeping, at this hour in their comfy beds.

Frankie didn't know how he was going to face working, especially when he felt this tired. Why did his father have to start so early? If he heard his dad say 'the early bird catches the worm' one more time, he was going to scream!

They arrived at the Harry's Homes workshop late,

due to Frankie's sleep-in. Harry's other employees took great delight in the fact their boss was late, for the first time ever.

"What time do you call this Harry?" one worker laughed.

"Had a bit of trouble rousing this one from his beauty sleep." replied Harry.

The other workers had been informed already that Frankie had joined their crew, as a punishment for his bad behaviour.

"Maybe this will make him think twice about playing games that give us sparrows a bad name." said the worker.

Frankie tried not to blush.

Frankie was small, even for a sparrow, but he more than made up for his lack of height. He was lightning fast and, even though most of the teachers at school never thought so, he was very intelligent. However, he was also always in trouble and, this time, he was paying the price.

Frankie was to help his father build a nest for a lovely little family of starling's right next to the Bird Stop Cafe. His job was to fetch and carry things his father needed to build the nest.

"I want you to keep bringing a steady supply of branches Frankie and I don't want any of them broken. Oh … and bring plenty of berries as well." Harry said.

"What are the berries for?" Frankie asked.

"To stop me from getting hungry!" said Harry.

Frankie had barely started gathering the branches his father needed but he found he was already exhausted. The combination of his interrupted sleep and the hard work left him tired and sore. His whole body ached. There was only one thing that could help him.

He decided to take a sneaky nap in the trees, just for five minutes or so …

CHAPTER 6
Stop! Thief!

"What do you mean, 'you lost him'?" Pratchett screamed at Jeff Robin.

"He knew he was being followed. Then, he saw how small I am, and he started chasing me. I only just managed to get away."

"You *only just managed to get away?* You were meant to follow *him*! Hopeless! Absolutely hopeless, that's what you are."

It was at exactly that moment that the magpie they had been looking for appeared behind Pratchett.

"Detec …"

"I can't believe I gave you a simple job and you couldn't even do that properly! Why on earth do I put up with you?"

"But he …"

"I suppose I should blame myself for relying on

someone who clearly isn't up to the job. But that's what I get for giving…"

"He, he, he …"

"… a bird like you a second chance. What is it? What are you twittering on about?"

"He … he's right behind you." Jeff spluttered.

"Well, why didn't you say? Out of the way! Let the professional handle this."

The little robin looked up to the sky, exasperated.

"Stop there! I want a word with you. Remain where you are!" Pratchett shouted.

However, the magpie wasn't for hanging around. He'd discovered who was after him, and it was even worse than he feared. He scrambled to get away from Pratchett.

"Stop! Thief!"

The magpie had planned on speaking to Jeff Robin, to find out why he was following him. Now that he realised it was all down to Pratchett, there was no way he was hanging around for an explanation. Pratchett was Trouble with a capital T, and nothing good could come from speaking with him, especially when he was yelling 'thief'.

The magpie flew for all he was worth. He knew he

was faster than Pratchett, and the police-pigeon's little helper didn't look so keen to give chase anymore. There was no way he would be caught. Pratchett was trailing behind and already looked out of puff. Why did Pratchett want to catch him in any case? He hadn't done anything wrong, so why was he being branded a thief? The magpie wasn't stopping to find out. He flew even faster, and would be away scot free any second. Little did he know, a young sparrow was about to bring the police chase to a halt.

Frankie was having a lovely dream – (Mr Finch was being arrested by the Pigeon Police for giving his class too much homework), – when the commotion of the chase startled him awake. He heard the shouts from Detective Pratchett and then saw a large magpie hurtling towards him. Instinctively, Frankie grabbed his father's long nest-building pole and hooked it around the magpie's talon. It was a one-in-a-million shot, but it worked. The magpie spiralled out of control, only stopping when a large oak tree got in his way.

The magpie lay dazed at the bottom of the tree, seeing stars.

The chase was over and it was all down to the quick thinking of Frankie Sparrow.

CHAPTER 7

Interview with a Fidget

The large scruffy magpie walked up and down the length of the interview room. He couldn't keep still. Johnny Fidget was his name, and it was apt.

"Sit down Fidget!" Detective Pratchett commanded, upon his entry to the room.

Fidget reluctantly sat, but still looked as if he had ants in his pants.

"Right, let's get this interview done and dusted. We both know you are going to confess …" Pratchett was cut off in mid flow when the door to the interview room opened.

"Detective Pratchett, you don't mind if I sit in do you?" It was Detective Doolan. Without waiting for an answer, he entered the room and grabbed a chair. Pratchett didn't look so smug anymore.

"Err, no. That's fine, Sir. No problem at all."

"Good, good. Fire away, then." Doolan said.

Pratchett now had one thing in common with Johnny Fidget, both of them looked like they couldn't sit still, now.

"Can you …Err, I mean … How many times have you been arrested now for nest-breaking, Mr Fidget?" Pratchett asked the magpie. He hadn't expected supervision on the interview and was trying to regain his composure. This wasn't the way it was supposed to go.

"You know I've been arrested a few times because you happen to be the one who arrested me. That was a long time ago, though. I've changed my ways since then and I didn't do this!" Fidget stood as he spoke. He was clearly more agitated than usual.

"Sit down Johnny! We both know I caught you red-handed three times before. I've caught you again this time. Now, do yourself a favour: admit to breaking into the owl nests and we'll try and come to some sort of arrangement."

"I can't admit something I didn't do!" Fidget protested.

"Well case closed! The truthful magpie says he didn't do it, so we must believe him! Tell me this, then, Fidget: Why did you fly away so quickly when you saw me coming?" Pratchett was standing, now.

"I'm always in a rush to get everywhere! Plus, I saw you and thought you were going to frame me for something I didn't do. If you must know, I was actually heading to the Police Nest, because I was scared-"

"Scared! You *should* be scared, Fidget!" Pratchett shouted.

"OK, OK! Let's all calm down here. Mr Fidget, you say we've got the wrong bird and Detective Pratchett thinks otherwise, so we'll have to look into it further. Does that sound fair to you both?" Detective Doolan intervened. He had seen enough and was glad he sat in on the interview. If Pratchett was like this with him here, what would he have been like if he was alone with the suspect?

"I had nothing to do with any nest robberies. Honestly, Mr Doolan." Fidget said.

"**We'll find proof you did this, Fidget. Mark my words**!" Pratchett screamed. He stormed from the room, leaving the door almost hanging off its hinges.

CHAPTER 8

Uncle Charlie Sparrow

Uncle Charlie Sparrow was having a nap in his office. Not because he was tired, but because he had nothing else to do. There had been quiet spells before, of course, but nothing as bad as this.

Once upon a time, Charlie Sparrow had dreamed of joining the Pigeon Police. When he went to apply, however, the pigeons made it clear that sparrows were not welcome on the force. After they grew tired of his begging, they let him take the tests. To his embarrassment, he failed every one. Charlie had let himself go. His vision had been deteriorating for a while. The pigeons were right, in the end – he wasn't cut out for the police.

Setting up on his own as a Private Investigator was the next best thing. Or so he had thought. It had been one disaster after another, and to say business was slow was an understatement. The main problem was that he simply did not solve cases. If truth be told he was thinking about giving it all up.

Charlie was roused from his nap when the office phone chirped.

"Hi Charlie." It was his brother, Harry- "How's business these days?"

"Never better! I'm rushed off my feet here." Charlie lied.

"Excellent! Maybe I can help you out. I've got a favour to ask."

"Ask away, Harry."

"I've had Frankie working with me on the nests, but it's not for him. He's got it into his head that he wants to work as an investigator. Like his favourite uncle. He helped the police catch a magpie today and now he thinks he'd be good at catching criminals. I was wondering if he might be able to help you with your heavy workload"

"Of course. No problem at all! Send him 'round tomorrow, 7am sharp. I'll show him the ropes." Charlie agreed, without hesitation. Maybe that's exactly what was needed: an extra pair of wings around the place.

"As easy as that? I thought you'd say 'no'?" Harry was bemused. He'd planned to tell his son there was no chance Charlie would have him. His brother had agreed far too easily.

"If Frankie thinks' he's got the Investigator Bug, of course he can help me out."

"It's set, then, I'll make sure he's there in the morning. Thanks, Charlie." Harry put the phone down, immediately regretting his decision to make the call. What sort of dad allowed his son to go to work as a Private Detective?

CHAPTER 9

Framing the Fidget

"It's simple," the large bird said. "Just keep to the plan. If Fidget gets the blame then no one will come looking for us. Or more importantly, no one will come looking for me. He's done this before and I don't believe for one second that he's reformed. A leopard can't change its spots! We just need to make sure the right evidence is in place so there's no doubt of his guilt. We can sort that out, no worries."

"But …he didn't do this. He's innocent!" The small bird protested.

"Do you want to get caught? Do you want to lose everything you've ever worked for? All because you care about poor, *trustworthy,* Fidget?"

There was no reply.

"Have you seen the state of Fidget's nest? We're doing him a favour, putting him in jail. At least he'll have a proper roof over his head. Plus, he'll get six meals a day. It looks like he could do with the food."

"What are we going to do?" the small bird asked, nervously.

"Don't look so worried! We're not stealing anything else. I simply want you to enter his nest and place these papers in the bedroom. Stash them under the bed and then get out as fast as you can. Whatever you do, don't let anyone see you."

The small bird agreed, reluctantly, to do as he was told. He feared for his safety if he didn't.

He was good at this job. He broke in the magpie's nest with ease, and without drawing any attention to himself. Nobody would ever know there had been a forced entry, the door wasn't even locked properly, in any case. The place was an absolute mess but, thankfully, nobody was at home. The small bird made his way through the living room, into the bedroom. It was tiny and in urgent need of repair. He crept towards the bed and placed the papers under it. Then he turned and left, as quickly and quietly as he had entered. No one saw him come or go.

"Job done." said the small bird.

"I told you there was nothing to worry about."

"That's the last time I'm ever doing anything like that."

"You'll do what I tell you to do, or there will be consequences!"

The large bird yanked the small bird's glasses from his face and smashed them with his large beak. The little bird was horrified.

"This time it's your glasses. Next time you might not be so lucky!" The large bird threw the ruined glasses into the sky and flew away.

CHAPTER 10
Frankie's first day

Uncle Charlie Sparrow's office was a leisurely five minute flight from Frankie's family home, in a large tree located in a little old lady's garden. Frankie had visited before, with his father and liked it there. Old Mrs Campbell had a bird feeder, which was kept well stocked, and she often ate cake outside, dropping crumbs all over the lawn. There was always plenty of food, (maybe a little too much food judging by the size of his Uncle), in Old Mrs Campbell's garden.

Most birds thought of Uncle Charlie as "mildly eccentric", and he certainly did appear that way to those who did not know him. He dressed very oddly, in bright, clashing colours, and he always wore lurid bow-ties. He was overweight, for a sparrow, and wore big round glasses that were kept on his face by a rubber band. Despite his peculiar appearance, he was a kind, gentle soul. He had always been good to Frankie. He would do anything for his little nephew.

"Things are a bit quiet around here just now. But don't you worry - it'll pick up. It almost always does. With your assistance, we will definitely solve the next case!" Charlie didn't sound completely convincing.

"This can be your desk here. I want you to keep things nice and tidy." Charlie showed Frankie to a small area, which was as far from "nice and tidy" as Frankie could imagine. Piles of paper were strewn all over the place.

"This is where the case files go." Charlie pointed to the table. Files were stacked in teetering towers. There was no order to anything.

"Your cleaner on strike just now Uncle Charlie?" Frankie laughed.

"That can be your first job, organising the files into some sort of order. I'll go and sort myself a wee snack and you can make a start. Sound's fair to me!"

Frankie wasn't laughing anymore. This is not what he had signed up for. He was looking forward to high-speed bird chases and catching dangerous criminals, not cleaning up after his messy uncle. However, just as he was about to get started with tidying, the office phone began to tweet. Charlie leapt to answer it.

"Charlie …I mean, Private Detective Sparrow,

speaking. How can I help you?" Charlie stuttered, pacing up and down as he spoke. He listened for a moment to the caller, suddenly looking very excited.

"Yes! Oh, not a problem. We'll get on the case! We'll find him. Loads of cases like this one … That's great! We'll drop everything and get on it right away. In fact our new detective will … Absolutely. Don't you worry!" Charlie looked positively gleeful.

"This is no coincidence! We're going to solve this one! No coincidence at all."

"What's happening Uncle Charlie?" Frankie asked, as his uncle hung up the phone.

"Oh, right! Sorry, I'm not used to having anyone else in the office. That was the head teacher of your school … Don't look so worried. It wasn't about you! A teacher at the school has disappeared! He didn't turn up for the holiday classes. Isn't it great? And, on the very same day you come to work with me, *we* get the call to find him! It's no coincidence, I tell you! We're *destined* to solve this case! Destined!"

"What teacher is it?" Frankie asked, a sinking feeling in his belly telling him that he already knew the answer.

"It's a Mr Finch. You know him?"

"You could say that."

The case of the missing schoolteacher had begun.

CHAPTER 11
The set up

The Pigeon Detectives assembled outside the Police Nest. Detective Doolan briefed his troops. They were going to search Johnny Fidget's nest.

"Detective Pratchett, I think it would be wise if you stayed here today, just so there is no suggestion of anything … *untoward,* happening." Doolan said.

"What? First you want to interview Fidget because you don't trust me to do it myself and now you don't want me at the search! What do you think I'll do? Plant something? Go! Search the place! I don't need to be there to know Fidget is guilty!" Pratchett was actually much calmer than he appeared. He knew a straight-laced cop like Doolan wouldn't let him anywhere near the search. It didn't matter, though. It was only a matter of time before the evidence needed to put Fidget behind bars was found. Even Doolan and his hopeless team couldn't fail to find it.

Doolan and his team arrived at Johnny Fidget's nest. It was in a sorry state - the shabbiest nest in the worst part of town. The whole place looked in need of urgent repair. The front door didn't even have a proper lock - it was held together by the flimsiest of branches. Rain water leaked in through several large holes in the roof.

The Pigeon Police entered, while Fidget and Doolan watched on from outside. Fidget knew there was nothing in there that would incriminate him. His days of crime were well and truly behind him. He had learned his lesson and was thankful that this search would finally clear his name. However, he found himself unable to be completely at peace. There was something niggling away at him.

He sensed that everything might not work out as it should.

"Detective Doolan, I think I've found something." shouted one of the Pigeon Detectives after a few minutes inside. He was holding a pile of papers high. Fidget began to feel truly nervous.

Doolan made his way over to the Detective.

"Let's take a look." Doolan took his time checking over the evidence, then made his way back outside.

"I told you there's nothing to find." Fidget said, on

Doolan's arrival. However, he sensed that something wasn't right. The expression on the pigeon's face was unsettling him.

"That's where you're wrong, Mr Fidget, I'm afraid we found a file of papers inside. They were stolen from a member of the Owl Parliament a few days ago."

"No way! How can this be? I've been framed! That's the only explanation! Where did you find them?" Fidget was even more animated than usual. His worst fears had been realised.

"They were under your bed. They weren't even hidden very well. I gave you the benefit of the doubt but I'm afraid your guilt is here for all to see. Take him away please." Doolan had doubted that Fidget was the culprit, but the evidence proved him wrong. Pratchett had been right all along.

"Honestly, Mr Doolan! I'm innocent! I never did this!" Fidget shouted as he was led back to the Police Nest.

The nest robber had been caught once and for all, so why was Detective Doolan still not happy?

CHAPTER 12

Frankie Sparrow on the case

"This is the perfect case for us, Frankie. Mr Finch hasn't been seen since the last day of term. He was meant to be teaching at the holiday school but hasn't turned up. You can help us find out who he was friendly with at school and what he was like as a person." Charlie bounced up and down with excitement.

"This can be your first lesson: 'how to interview a witness'."

"Okay." Frankie said, feeling an excited buzz of his own. This was more like it!

"What's this Mr Finch like?" Charlie asked.

"He keeps me back for detention at least once a week. He's the strictest, nastiest, meanest teacher in our school. We call him 'Fearsome Finchy', although, not to his face. Sparky got caught calling him that once and was given detention for a week."

"I know the mischief you get up to Frankie so I'm sure he has reasons for keeping you back after school. Thing is, though, your head teacher says it's out of character for Mr Finch to go missing like this, so the question is: what's happened to him?"

"I don't know." Frankie admitted.

"There you go! That's how you interview a witness." Charlie said.

"That's it? That's the only question's you're going to ask?"

"Err … no. Of course not."

Frankie was beginning to understand why his uncle's business was so quiet.

"Why don't you ask me about the last time I saw him? What he was up to?" Frankie said.

"I was just coming to that! So …when was the last time you saw him and what was he up to?"

"It was the last day of term - the day he went missing. I was kept back, as usual, for absolutely nothing. When I left Mr Finch was still there. He was on the phone almost the whole time I was with him. It sounded like he was trying to book a holiday."

"A holiday?"

"Yeah, I overheard him talking about flights."

"Interesting." Charlie said, pacing up and down.

"I don't know what's happened to him, though." Frankie said.

"Neither do I, but I will tell you one thing: by hook or by crook we're going to find out.

*

Frankie and Charlie decided to start the hunt for Mr Finch at the Sparrow school, as it was the last place he had been seen alive and well. It was early in the morning, so the teachers hadn't arrived yet for the holiday school. The building was being opened by the janitor - a friendly pigeon called Clarence. Clarence had worked at Sparrow Junior High for more years than he cared to remember.

"Excuse me, sir. May I have a quick word with you about a member of staff here? My name's Charlie Sparrow and I'm a Private Investigator. This is my nephew, Frankie. He's helping me out. I've been asked to help find a Mr Finch. I was wondering if you could tell us anything about the last time you saw him." Charlie hadn't planned on asking the janitor any questions but he was the only one around and it couldn't do any harm.

"Good to see you staying out of trouble, Frankie. The last time I saw Mr Finch would have been the same as you - the last day of term. I was hoping to get away early that day but, because detention was on, I couldn't leave." Clarence laughed heartily, directing a wink at Frankie.

"Err ... I'm really sorry about that." Frankie said.

"Mr Finch left school after detention had finished. No ... I tell a lie - he was delayed further, that day, I remember because he kept me waiting another half an hour to lock the place up. My Irene was furious when I was late."

"Thanks for your help." Charlie said, considering the conversation over.

"Do you know why he was late in leaving?" Frankie pressed.

"He had a visitor and told me he didn't want to be disturbed down in his lab. Mr Finch is the science teacher here, as you probably know. Now that you mention it, he seemed on edge, that night. He looked as if he had a lot on his mind, when he eventually left."

Charlie started to walk away again but Frankie had one final question: "You don't happen to know who Mr Finch's visitor was?"

"I'm afraid not. He was a big bird, though, - a pigeon, like myself, but much larger than I am. Looked as though he could have been police, but I couldn't be sure. I do remember one thing though, he wore a ridiculous flat cap and was as rude as they come. Barged right past me on his way out."

Charlie knew all about Frankie's adventure with the magpie. He also knew all about the ungrateful Pigeon Detective, called Pratchett, who was rude and wore a flat cap. The two sparrow's looked at each other. Why would Detective Pratchett be visiting Mr Finch?

CHAPTER 13

Peggy Beans

Peggy Beans was deep in thought. It was midnight, but she was wide awake. She always was at this hour. Peggy was an owl and, as you know, owls live their lives in the night-time. Peggy Beans was not just any ordinary owl, though. She was the head of the Owl Parliament, and that meant she was the most important bird there was.

Peggy and her colleagues in the Parliament were tasked with overseeing the Pigeon Detective leadership contest. The contest was happening very soon, and Peggy would face a tough decision. She liked the current leader, Detective Doolan. He was a nice pigeon. He had never caused any problems before. Crime had always been under control with him in charge, but recently that had changed. These blasted nest robberies were causing her no end of problems. Five of her owl colleagues had found themselves victims of the break-ins. The Parliament were not best pleased. There was only so long that Peggy could fob off their complaints. Some of them wanted poor Detective Doolan sacked. They thought he wasn't up to the job any more. Peggy was convinced it would resolve, but in the meantime, the grievances were mounting. She had even received an objection from a member of the Pigeon Police, themselves. The anonymous letter asserted that Doolan had no idea what he was doing. That he was an incompetent fool and should be given early retirement. One thing was for sure, this whole business was a headache she could well do without.

Peggy hoped that her meeting with the Pigeon Detective leader would be a positive one. The last thing she wanted was to have to tell him he was being replaced.

Detective Doolan arrived for their chat with a spring in his step.

"Good evening, Detective. Thanks for coming at such a late hour." Peggy said.

"Not a problem. Especially as I have good news! We have arrested the nest robber!"

"I can't tell you how happy I am to hear you say that!"

"It's a weight off my feathers, I can tell you!" said Doolan.

"What good timing, with the election just about to start. We owls were getting very concerned."

"I understand that. Thankfully, there is no more need to worry. The robberies are at an end."

Peggy Beans didn't have the heart to tell Doolan that the owls were pressuring her to replace him and, if the nest robber hadn't been caught, he would have been sacked. She liked Detective Doolan, but even some of her closest friends in the Parliament wanted a change of leadership. Their opinion was that change might come in the form of the newest election candidate: a certain detective called Paulie Pratchett.

CHAPTER 14

Poor Fidget

Johnny Fidget paced frantically, up and down in his jail cell.

He couldn't believe what had happened.

He had been in trouble before, it was true, but he had tried hard to change.

He *had* changed.

He had even landed himself a job, for the first time ever. Yet, here he was, stuck in a jail cell for something he didn't do.

Magpies had a bad reputation. When something went missing, or something was stolen, people blamed the magpie. He couldn't deny that it was deserved, sometimes, but not all magpies should be tarred by the same brush. There were good magpies, as well as bad.

Question's turned over and over in Fidget's head:

Who had framed him for the nest robberies and, just as importantly, – *why*?

He couldn't work it out. So, here he was: pacing up and down, left and right.

He was even beginning to doubt himself. Maybe he deserved this, for all his wrongdoing in the past?

Poor Fidget was in a terrible state.

The pigeons had provided food for him, but he was far too stressed to eat. He was fading away.

How was he going to prove his innocence when everyone was so convinced he was the culprit?

How was he going to prove his innocence, when he was stuck here in this tiny jail cell?

CHAPTER 15
Miles

Frankie and Charlie arrived at the Flying Station early the next morning. Frankie had heard Mr Finch talking on the phone, talking about booking flights. He wanted to see if there was anyone who had seen him, and to search for anything that could help him, and Uncle Charlie, find the missing teacher.

The station was busy. It was the school holidays. Families were flying out on holiday, and the place was bustling with birds of all species.

Music played through a loud speaker:

'Come fly with me, come fly, let's fly away ...'

Occasionally, the music was interrupted by a passenger announcement:

'Passenger Harley Swallow, please make your way to gate 3. Your pilot is ready for take-off! That's Passenger Harley Swallow, gate 3.'

Charlie made his way over to the dining area, where he knew the pilots ate. He was looking for a friend of his. The friend was a pilot, who would no doubt be fuelling up before a long-haul flight. Charlie spotted him perched in front of an absolutely massive breakfast.

"Morning, Miles. OK if we have a little chat?" Miles was a huge seagull, who was greedily wolfing down a full breakfast and a bowl of worms - at the same time it seemed. 'Miles' had earned his nickname from his profession - he was a pilot who carried smaller birds on long journeys. He flew all over the country. Perhaps due to his strenuous job, Miles loved his grub. He loved it almost as much as he loved to talk.

"Of course, Charlie boy. I don't know if I'll be able to help, but I'll give it a go. You know me - always ready to lend a helping claw, if I can." Miles spoke very quickly, Charlie and Frankie struggled to keep up.

"Do you happen to remember seeing a passenger called Mr Finch, over the past few days?" Charlie pulled out a photo of Mr Finch. It was taken from

Frankie's school yearbook.

Miles put down his bowl. It was still overflowing. He studied the photo.

"It's been very busy the past few days, because of these school holidays – too many holidays if you ask me! Jam-packed, it's been, - everyone flying out, here, there and everywhere. Funny thing - I was getting ready to fly on Friday but my flight was delayed. A passenger never turned up on time. Turns out it was your missing Mr Finch here." Miles tapped the photo.

"We give birds a ten minute window, but if they don't show by then, well, that's tough. We go without them. Finch never showed up until I was ready to take-off. He made it with seconds to spare. He apologised for his lateness, but I was in a bit of a hurry, so I wasn't having any of his apology. Anyway, he hopped on board, and I flew him and the rest of the party. I do remember that he looked a bit flustered. In fact, he said he'd lost his glasses. That's why he was so late." Miles loved to talk, Charlie and Frankie could hardly get a word in.

"Did you talk to Mr Finch? Where did you drop him?" Miles finally took a breath, giving Charlie a chance to ask his question.

"Talk to him? Oh, yes. I'll tell you exactly what I said to him! I gave him a right ear-bashing. I said, 'You listen here, and you listen good! What time do you call this Mr Finch? You're nine minutes past my departure time, and you're keeping all these good folks back! You're also making me late, and I hate being late. It makes me look lazy not to mention -"

"Miles!" Charlie interrupted. "We're in a bit of a rush, here, so if you could keep it to the main facts ..." Miles could talk for days, and, by the sounds of it, today he was in an especially talkative mood. The two investigators could be there for hours, unless one of them intervened.

"OK, I'll cut to the chase. I gave Finch a talking-to because he was late. He apologised and said he was delayed because he had lost his glasses. He could hardly see three talons in front of him and looked in a bit of a state - I asked if he was good to fly. He said he was fine. I dropped him off with the rest of the passengers. They were all excited because they were getting away on a wee holiday. Lucky-so-and-so's! No holidays for big Miles here. I've not been on holiday since back in ... When was it now? Let me think ... Must be near on three years ... No, make that four ..."

"Miles! This is all great stuff, but if you could tell me where you dropped off Mr Finch, that would be fantastic. We can be on our way, then. Let you get on with your breakfast."

"Oh, all right. Sorry, Charlie. I was going on a bit, wasn't I? I dropped Finch and the rest of them off at Dunterley Point. He was treating himself to a stay at one of the luxury nests. All right for some! He was staying in the top apartment, as well, I saw his booking. I'd love nothing more than to put my feet up and have a wee holiday, but no rest for the wicked, eh?"

"That's great. Thanks for your help, Miles" Charlie said.

"No problem. Any time. I do like our little chats!"

"Just one last thing. Who were the rest of the passengers on Mr Finch's flight?" Frankie asked.

"I'm glad you asked. There was the Robinson family - lovely little bunch they are. Always so polite! Then there was the Wilkerson's, and there were two passengers who came along for the journey by themselves. Mr Finch was one, who you know. And then there was a small pigeon … Haggs I think he was called. Didn't talk to him much. He seemed to keep himself to himself. Although, now I come to think of it, he was quite interested in your Mr Finch. He followed on after him." Miles chuckled away to himself.

"Thanks very much, Miles. You've been a great help." Charlie said.

Miles had given the sparrows plenty to think about.

CHAPTER 16

The Press Conference

"Detective Pratchett! Could I have a word?" Doolan asked.

"Of course."

"I just want to congratulate you on catching the nest robber, and apologise for having doubted you."

"Not a problem, Boss." Pratchett smiled.

"We'll be having a press conference to announce that the robber has been caught and since it was all down to you, it would only be right if you were to stand alongside me when I make the announcement. I trust this is OK with you?"

"No problem at all, but don't be giving me all of the credit. It was a team effort. What am I saying? Of course it wasn't a team effort! Let's be honest, if it wasn't for me, then who knows how long this might have continued?"

"Yes I suppose you're right- Well done again Detective Pratchett. Sterling work."

Pratchett flew away leaving Doolan behind with his deputy, Detective Twittery. She was a pigeon who didn't suffer fools gladly. She had never liked Detective Pratchett.

"I can't believe you apologised to him. We both know something's not right here." Detective Twittery said.

"I wouldn't have believed it, if I hadn't seen it with my own eyes, but the evidence was there in Fidget's nest. Pratchett wasn't even on the search. I may not like him or his methods, but on this occasion, it looks like we were wrong."

"I'm telling you. Something stinks about this!"

*

The flashes from the cameras were dazzling.

Detectives Doolan and Pratchett took their seats in front of the newspaper-birds.

Detective Doolan addressed the audience.

"Member's of the public, and members of the press, thank you very much for coming along today. The reason for this press conference is to announce some fantastic news. I will keep you in suspense no longer -"

"The nest robber has been caught!" Pratchett interrupted.

"Yes, Detective Pratchett here is right. The nest -" Doolan attempted to resume.

"And I was the pigeon who caught him!" Pratchett blurted.

"Yes, as I was saying, the nest robber has been caught and we would like to congratulate the team - and particularly Detective Pratchett - on a job well done."

"I'll take it from here, Detective Doolan. I'm sure you all have questions on how I captured the thief, so, ask away!" Pratchett interrupted, yet again. Doolan looked furious at this turn of events.

The birds in the assembled media began firing questions at Pratchett, who revelled in the limelight.

"How did I catch him, when all others failed? Was that the question?" It wasn't.

"Well, let me tell you this - Detective Pratchett does not stop until he has caught his bird. I'm not like the rest of the Pigeon Detectives who go back home after a shift and forget all about their work. No, no, no! I eat, sleep and breathe this job. I didn't rest until I caught the guilty bird." Pratchett was loving the attention.

"Who was the guilty bird?" someone shouted.

"I'm glad you asked! A horrible magpie, by the name of Johnny Fidget. Thought he was getting away with it, as well! Didn't reckon he'd encounter Detective Paulie Pratchett, though, did he?"

"Thank you, everyone for attending this short press conference. As you know, we're all very busy, trying to keep crime down, and so we must get back." Doolan ended the press conference, hastily.

It had been a disaster.

He never should have invited Pratchett along.

CHAPTER 17
Swifty the Gadget

"A stakeout! That's the only thing for it Frankie."
Charlie said. "We have to watch the nests at Dunterley
Point and, hopefully, spot Mr Finch. We need some
tools, first, and I know just the bird to sort us out."

They were on their way to see Charlie's friend,
"Swifty the Gadget". Swifty stayed close to the
ground, because he couldn't fly any more (due to a
horrible incident with a cat). He now used all sorts of
clever gadgets to help him stay safe. This was the
reason for his nickname.

"If you want to carry out effective surveillance
missions, you have to visit the Gadget." Charlie said.

The two sparrows knocked on Swifty's door, which
was hidden away behind some thick bushes. There was
no answer.

"I don't know where Swifty could be. He's

normally in at this hour."

Just at that second, the trees ruffled and, from out of nowhere, a voice was heard.

"I'm getting good at the old camouflage game, if even big Charlie Sparrow can't spot me!"

"I still can't spot you!" Charlie laughed. There was no sign of the old bird they had come to visit. Suddenly, there was a loud bang. Smoke rose all around them and, appearing from the middle of it, there was Swifty the Gadget! He was also covered in leaves.

Swifty coughed and spluttered. "I need to stop doing that! Not got the lungs for it any more, but it scares off cats like nobody's business! How can I help you fine sparrows then? I presume you need help, because that's the only time I see Charlie boy, here." Swifty laughed.

"We're trying to track down a bird and we need some supplies for a stakeout. I immediately thought of you."

"You know I'll always help you out. Let me have a look." The swift disappeared into his heavily camouflaged nest and, after two minutes of banging and clanging, reappeared with an old battered case.

"Let's see what we have for you. How's about some nice camouflage? Well, that's a given. I can give you some lovely binoculars ....Oh, and this. You'll love this - a state of the art listening device."

"That sounds great to me."

"What's this case you're on, anyway?"

"We're on the lookout for a missing teacher. He works at the Sparrow school."

"Spit it out, Charlie! What's this teacher's name?"

"Oh yes. Sorry, I thought I had mentioned him. It's a Mr Finch."

"Finch! I remember him. Great woodwork teacher. I've spoken to him a few times. We used to stay in the same trees, before my accident."

"What did you say? He teaches woodwork?"

"Yes, that's Finch all right. Best woodwork teacher there is."

CHAPTER 18

The Election begins ...

The Owl Parliament Nest was a magnificent site. It had taken twenty sparrows well over a month, working non-stop to complete it. It took up the whole of a large birch tree. There were around forty nests, where the entire Parliament of Owl's lived when Parliament was in session, and a huge grand hall. This was where tonight's meeting was to take place. With the owls, all of the important business happened in the night-time.

Peggy Beans was in the grand hall, sitting at the head of the long top table, which was adorned with candles of various shapes and sizes. She called the meeting to order.

"Good evening. Let me begin by saying 'thank you' to everyone, for your attendance at this meeting. Now, without further ado, let's get down to business." Peggy didn't like to waste time. "The position of Pigeon Detective leader is a very important post. Tonight, we are announcing the candidates who are up for election."

"There are three great candidates: Detective Doolan, as you all know, is seeking re-election. Detective Twittery, who you also know as deputy, is seeking a move up in the ranks. And we have a new candidate, who is standing for the very first time - Detective Paulie Pratchett."

Doolan looked stunned. Pratchett was standing against him to become leader?

"Each of the candidates will now make a short speech, to outline why they believe they are worthy of your vote. First up, let's have the newcomer to the process. Please give a round of applause for Detective Pratchett."

"Thank you, Miss Beans. I'm afraid to say that Detective Doolan, nice chap that he is, is not up to the job of leading the Pigeon Police anymore. Nest robberies are at an all-time high, and important members of this very Parliament have been targeted. Detective Doolan had no idea where to begin the investigation, whereas I, Detective Paulie Pratchett, solved the case using good old-fashioned police work. If it wasn't for me, the robber would still be at large.

Who knows what other terrible things could have happened! Esteemed members of the Owl Parliament could have been hurt, kidnapped, or even killed! In my view, there is only one bird capable of leading this force, and that bird is the one and only Detective Paulie Pratchett."

Doolan stood, watching the stage, absolutely aghast. Pratchett had done the dirty on him. He lost himself in his rage, and was only summoned back to action by Peggy Beans shouting his name. It was his turn to make a speech to the Parliament. He had to compose himself. He had even missed Detective Twittery's speech.

"Sorry, folks. I was just a little stunned by Detective Pratchett's statement. I have a great record as leader. I would like to continue with my role, as I feel I have a lot more to achieve. Thank you."

Doolan had prepared a longer speech but, Pratchett's pronouncements had thrown him completely off course. He could hardly contain how angry he was - not just at Pratchett but, also, at himself.

How could he have been fooled so easy?

Peggy Beans took to the microphone, again, and duly announced the election open. "There will now be three days of voting. We will gather here again, after this period, to announce the result. Good night to you all."

CHAPTER 19

The Stakeout

"I can't believe we didn't know Mr Finch was the woodwork teacher, before he taught science."

"Is it a big deal?" Frankie asked, still not grasping the significance of this revelation.

"Well, let's think about it: there have been all sorts of nest robberies, lately, and, from what I hear no sign of forced entry was found. Finch is, apparently, the best woodwork teacher around, and just happens to go missing at the same time all of this is going on. It all seems a bit fishy to me. I'd bet my bottom dollar on it: Mr Finch is the one breaking into the nests."

"No way! Mr Finch would never do anything that was against the law." said Frankie.

"Maybe he's being forced into it, though …"

*

Frankie and Charlie perched in the tree nearest to Mr Finch's nest at Dunterley Point. Miles told them that he was staying on the top floor. They were lovely, luxury nests, in a large tree that overlooked the park. The two sparrows were camouflaged by all of the extra leaves and twigs they had acquired from Swifty. They watched the nest through his special binoculars. The listening equipment was set up outside the nest. Frankie had also enlisted the help of his friend, Sparky, who was positioned a couple of miles away. Frankie had a walkie-talkie set up, so he could inform Sparky of anything or anyone coming his way. The walkie-talkie was basically a plastic cup with string that stretched for miles but it would do the job. They were determined not to miss a thing.

"This is the boring bit, Frankie. We'll watch the nest, see who comes and goes, then note it down. We might not find anything, but we might stumble upon something." Charlie spoke quietly. He was the cautious type. Frankie thought his uncle looked ridiculous, covered head-to-talons in leaves - especially as he still wore his bow tie. Today he had plumped for a bright red one.

Three hours into the stakeout and nothing had happened. Frankie didn't want to admit it, but he was bored. This was almost as bad as detention with Mr

Finch. He was right on the verge of falling asleep, when Uncle Charlie gave him a nudge. A small pigeon had arrived at Mr Finch's nest. He looked left, then right, and then repeated the action. He seemed extremely nervous. The small pigeon knocked on the door. No answer. The nest was empty. The shifty pigeon tried again, but still nobody responded. He tried to force the door open, but it didn't budge. He then pulled out a scrap of paper and hurriedly wrote something on it before sliding it through the post box and flying swiftly away.

"Pigeon of interest, coming your way, Sparky." Frankie said into his walkie-talkie.

"If only we could see what was written on that piece of paper." said Charlie.

"I can get it out." Frankie said before flying into action.

He used two long twigs to grasp the paper and, after a couple of minutes of manoeuvring, he managed to retrieve it.

"Well done Frankie!" Charlie said.

The two sparrows read over what was written on the paper:

"You better not cross us. We know where you are. Will all be over in 2 days."

The pigeon was obviously not Mr Finch's friend. The note was threatening him. It looked as though Charlie was right, after all: Mr Finch had landed himself in all sorts of trouble.

"We better find Mr Finch before other's do. It looks like he's in danger." said Charlie.

"Let's see where the pigeon got to. See if that helps us." said Frankie, picking up his walkie-talkie.

"Sparky, are you following the pigeon?"

There was no answer.

"Sparky, are you there?"

Still, there was nothing.

Only silence.

Frankie and Charlie flew to where Sparky was keeping lookout. Or, at least, where he *should* have been keeping lookout.

When they arrived, they found him fast asleep. They had missed their chance to follow the pigeon.

They had lost him.

CHAPTER 20

Charlie meets Peggy

Charlie Sparrow met with Peggy Beans at the Owl Parliament. He went to the meeting himself as it was late at night. Frankie was having some well-earned sleep, after hours spent on the surveillance mission. Charlie had known Peggy for as long as he could remember. They were good friends, and usually met for a meal and relaxed conversation. However, tonight, he was going to give her some bad news.

"Evening, Peggy. I hope you are well?"

"Yes, yes I'm as well as can be expected for an old bird." Peggy laughed. "I have a feeling that you're not here to enquire after my health, though. What's on your mind?"

"I'll just come out and say it: The Pigeon Police have got the wrong bird for the nest robberies."

"Oh, I think you must be mistaken Charlie. I saw

the evidence myself. Mr Fidget had the stolen Parliament papers in his nest."

"I don't think Fidget stole them, though. I believe he has been framed."

"Framed? I don't think so! Detective Doolan took measures to make sure that didn't happen."

"My nephew, Frankie, looked into the crimes Johnny Fidget committed, before this series. When Mr Fidget was caught, his break-ins were clumsy, and he left an absolute mess. The nest robberies, this time around, were carried out by a professional. There was no sign of forced entry; no mess whatsoever. These nest robberies were definitely undertaken by another bird. I'm sure of it. Mr Fidget is innocent."

"This is terrible news. The election closes in just two days. Detective Pratchett is the favourite to win, because he caught Mr Fidget, and now you're telling me he's put an innocent bird in jail? Oh, no. This is *dreadful* news."

"We believe that the disappearance of a teacher at the Sparrow School - a Mr Finch – is somehow linked to the nest robberies. We think that Finch is being forced to break into the nests. We think it was Mr *Finch,* and not Mr *Fidget,* who committed these crimes."

"Whoever could be forcing a teacher to do such a dreadful thing?"

"I'm not sure of that, yet, but one thing's for sure; the only bird benefitting from having Fidget in jail is now favourite to become Pigeon Detective leader."

"Oh, Charlie. This is terrible. Poor Detective Doolan! Poor Mr Fidget! I'll need to speak with the police and tell them of your concerns. What terrible timing. What a *mess*."

CHAPTER 21
The Bird Stop Cafe

The Bird Stop Cafe was a place where birds of all varieties came for a chat and a bite to eat. There were lots of tables and many comfy chairs so you could always get a seat. A songbird sang soothing melodies in the corner but was drowned out by the hustle and bustle of the busy eatery.

Mr Finch was a regular at the Bird Stop. He was still missing. Mr Fidget was also a regular, and he was lying in a jail cell.

"What can I get you two chaps, then?" the starling who owned the cafe asked Charlie and Frankie.

"We're not here for food, I'm afraid. We were hoping to ask you a couple of questions, about a friend of ours, and a regular of yours."

"No questions answered, until someone orders some food. I've got to make a living, after all." The cafe owner drove a hard bargain.

"Give us a slice of bread and some seeds, then." Charlie replied.

"That's more like it. Now, ask your two questions."

"Two questions?" Frankie said.

"A slice of bread and some seeds entitles you to two questions. If you ordered something a bit more substantial, then you could ask more." the starling said.

Charlie and Frankie exchanged a look. This starling was a tough nut.

"All right," Charlie said, slowly. "Maybe you could tell us if you know a Mr Finch. He's a teacher at the local school."

"Yes, I know him."

"Have you seen him recently?"

"Not for a week or so."

"How is he, when he comes in?"

"That's more than two questions. You'll need to order more than a bread slice if you want me to talk!" The cafe owner laughed.

"Give me a full sparrow breakfast, as well, then." Charlie conceded, grudgingly.

"Now we're talking! Take a seat and I'll be over with your food. Then, we can have a proper chat."

Five minutes passed, before the cafe owner

reappeared, carrying a plate piled high with food.

"Right, let me tell you about our Mr Finch," he said, taking a seat across from the two sparrows.

"He comes in here every day, sits at the same seat and has the same food. Didn't talk much to us. In fact, he always looked as though he was in a foul mood. Then, he *doesn't* come in, and I get you chaps asking after him. I get the police looking for him, too. It's all very mysterious."

"The police have been looking for him?" Charlie asked.

"Well, he never actually *said* he was police, but I knew right away. Not much gets by me. Knew he was police, the minute I clapped eyes on him."

"What did he ask you?"

"He asked if Finch was the type to talk a lot. Asked if he gossiped."

"Why were the police worried about Mr Finch talking?" Frankie asked the question this time.

"Who knows, young one. Maybe Finch knew something he shouldn't have known. Maybe he's been up to no good. You'd need to ask him that. If you ever find him, that is. The Police Pigeon looked happy, when I told him Finch barely says two words to anyone. I reckon it was the same Pigeon who stitched up a member of my staff for the owl nest robberies."

"A member of your staff?"

"Yeah, a magpie who was helping me out with the cleaning recently. Poor Johnny Fidget. Such a shame he got arrested. There's no way he carried out those robberies. He was never out of here, for a start, so I don't know where he would find the time! He was trying to turn his life around; put his criminal past behind him. I tried to help him out, as best I could. Sometimes, he was a little short to pay for his food, so I let him work here. In return, I kept him fed. In the end, he started working more regularly."

"Do you know the Pigeon Police bird's name?" Frankie asked.

"I don't think he gave me it. Massive pigeon, though, and he wore a ridiculous flat cap."

Charlie and Frankie exchanged a look. They knew exactly who the cafe owner's visitor had been.

Pratchett.

"Thanks for your help. We'll eat this and be on our way."

Charlie - who had already demolished a full breakfast, earlier in the day - was going to struggle to finish this one. He decided to give it a go anyway. As he was eating, a familiar face arrived. It was Miles.

"Miles! Good timing. Sit down and you can help me eat all of this!" Charlie called out.

Miles sat. He began to tuck into the plate of food, with enjoyment.

"I'm glad I bumped into you two. I've spotted the pigeon you were after - Mr Haggs." Miles said with his mouth full.

"Really? That's great news! Whereabouts is he?" Frankie asked.

Miles quickly finished the remaining food.

"Come with me. I'll show you."

CHAPTER 22
The Chase Is On!

Miles guided Charlie and Frankie outside, to where all of his passengers were waiting on him. They were being very patient. They knew how important it was for the pilot to be adequately fuelled.

"Jump on. I'll take you to where I saw our friend, Mr Haggs. My passengers won't mind a slight detour." The patient demeanours of the passengers began to waver, slightly.

Frankie and Charlie climbed, carefully, along with the other passengers, onto Miles' back. They grabbed a seat near the front. Charlie positioned himself so he could speak right into Miles' ear.

"Hold on tight, folks." Miles said before extending his huge wings and taking off.

He hadn't been flying for long, when he suddenly dived down into a tailspin. He came to a crashing halt.

"There you go! The one and only Haggs." He was right. Haggs was sitting in a tree, keeping watch on a nest ...

Mr Finch's nest.

Haggs seemed to know that something was up. He must have sensed he was being watched. Or heard Miles' failed attempt at a whisper.

Haggs hurriedly gathered his things. He set off at break-neck speed.

"Will I follow him, Charlie boy?" Miles asked, enthusiastically.

"What about your passengers?"

"They'll love it! Won't you folks?" Before the rest of the travellers could voice their disapproval, Miles pulled on his flying goggles. He set off in hot pursuit.

The chase was well and truly on!

The pigeon flew erratically. Miles followed a small distance behind, both birds travelling at speed.

"He's fast for a pigeon, but never fear! Miles won't lose him!"

The passengers clung onto their seats in terror. They were buffeted back and forth, one way and then the other.

Haggs flew at top speed, but Miles matched him all the way (whilst doing his best to try and keep a safe distance between them).

Haggs weaved in and out of trees, with Miles only moments behind. They both narrowly missed crashing, several times. It was far too close for comfort.

"He's going too fast!" shouted one passenger.

"We're going to crash!" shrieked another.

Miles wasn't listening though. He was enjoying the chase far too much.

He wasn't going to let Haggs get away.

"Stop in that large tree, just ahead. I think I know where our friend is going." Charlie shouted into Miles ear. He felt queasy from the turbulence. His glasses were askew and his bow-tie was spinning.

Miles did as he was told, but didn't seem to slow down any on his approach to the tree. In fact, it seemed as if he was speeding up! Everyone clung on for dear life! It looked, and felt, as though Miles was going to crash. At the very last second, he put on his brakes, and came to a shuddering halt. It was just as well all of the luggage was tied down. The same couldn't be said for his passengers. Each and every one of them was scared stiff, feathers dishevelled. At least one of the smaller birds was being sick over the side.

"Okie dokie, smokey! Let's do a wee bit of surveillance! Good fun, this detective lark, isn't it, folks?" Miles said, with glee, unaware that everyone else was in such a state.

This wasn't the best way to carry out surveillance. They weren't exactly camouflaged on the back of the big seagull, with eight other shaken, scruffy birds.

They all watched on, as the small pigeon stopped, looked left, looked right and then continued to his final destination:

The Police nest.

CHAPTER 23

Haggs slips up

Frankie and Charlie entered the Police nest.

There was no time to waste. They were going to confront Haggs.

"How can I help you?" the receptionist bird asked the two sparrows.

"We were wondering," Charlie asked, "- if we could have a word with the pigeon who flew in here just before us?"

"Detective Haggs?"

"Yes … *Detective* Haggs." Charlie replied.

"Two ticks and I'll get him down for you." The bird pressed a few buttons on the phone, before speaking quietly into the receiver.

After a few minutes of waiting, a door flew open and out stepped Detective Haggs. He really did not look at all happy to see them.

"Who are you and why have I been called away from my vital work to meet with you?" The small pigeon asked, he was in a foul mood right enough.

"Charlie and Frankie Sparrow. Private Investigators. We'd just like to ask you a couple of questions if you'd be so kind?"

"Questions? Go on then, I've not got all day, especially for sparrow Private Investigators!" Haggs scoffed.

"We're looking into the disappearance of a friend of ours - a teacher at the local school. Mr Finch is his name. We were wondering if you happened to know him."

"Never heard of him. Carrington Finch, you say? Never had the pleasure. Now anything else I can do for you? I'm a busy bird and can't stand twittering here all day." Haggs was shifty. He couldn't get rid of the two sparrows quickly enough.

"*Carrington* Finch?" said Frankie.

"Never heard of him. Now if you don't mind …" Haggs tried to usher them out.

"Carrington?" Charlie repeated. "Nobody said anything about his first name."

"You must have mentioned it."

"We didn't even know it."

"Lucky guess. Who knows? Who *cares?* I don't have

time for this nonsense. Good day to you. *'Sparrow Private Investigators'*, I ask you! Whatever next?" And, with that, Haggs flew quickly away.

"Mr Finch's first name is Carrington?" Frankie said, trying not to laugh.

"Well that proves Haggs knows him, and knows him well."

"But why would he say he *didn't* know him?" Frankie asked his uncle.

"Why indeed, young Frankie? Why indeed?"

CHAPTER 24

Pratchett begins to crack …

Mr Finch checked behind him, for what seemed like the twentieth time. He was getting used to being ultra-careful. He hated living like this, but felt he had no choice. He feared for his own safety, if either Pratchett or Haggs caught up with him. To make matters worse, he had heard there were two sparrows asking questions about him.

He knew the Pigeon Detective Leadership elections were closing shortly. He could return once they were completed and Pratchett was elected leader. Pratchett and Haggs would leave him alone, once they had what they wanted. Wouldn't they?

Finch's conscience was bothering him, though. He knew that the poor magpie was in jail. How could he live with himself knowing he'd played a part in putting an innocent bird behind bars? He was a teacher, for goodness sake! He was supposed to know right from wrong.

He needed to speak up, and he needed to do it soon.

He had to play his part in stopping all of this.

He had to make things right.

He was going to do it.

He had decided.

Mr Finch was going to stop Pratchett.

*

"Where can he be?" Pratchett asked Haggs.

"I couldn't find him at Dunterley Point. He has to be there, somewhere, though. I was on the same seagull flight, and he's not in the nest he booked. He's not in his home nest either. I've been watching it."

"You've let him get away! I told you not to let him out of your sight."

"I'm sorry, Paulie." Haggs bowed his head.

"'Sorry' is no good to me! What if he appears before the election result is announced, and ruins everything? You need to find him. Get to it."

However, Haggs didn't move.

"There's something else …" Haggs added, reluctantly.

"What is it?" Pratchett asked.

"There are Private Investigators sniffing around, asking questions. Sparrow Private Investigators."

"Sparrow Private Investigators! Asking questions about what?" Pratchett was even more furious now.

"They were asking about Mr Finch. They asked if I knew him," Haggs said.

"Please tell me you said you didn't?"

"Of course I said I didn't know him! I'm not that stupid. Although ..." Haggs stopped mid-sentence.

"What is it?" Pratchett asked.

"I might have let slip his first name - I'm sure they already knew it, and I think I covered it up well enough but ..."

Pratchett shook his head. Why could no-one do anything right?

"Why is it that, when things are finally coming together, you have to try and mess it up? I've had confirmation that the top job is mine. Nobody is going to ruin this for me. Not Finch, not Fidget, not you and especially not Sparrow Private Investigators!"

"What do you want me to do, Paulie?" Haggs asked.

"I want you to track down Finch and make sure he keeps quiet until after the election. And I want you to stop messing everything up. I'll make these sparrows disappear. Don't worry about that."

"I'll get right on it, Boss."

"In a few hours' time, voting closes, and I will be announced as Pigeon Detective leader. Nobody can stop me."

CHAPTER 25

Pratchett's Plot unravels

Peggy Beans set up a meeting at the Pigeon Police nest with Detective Doolan, straight after her chat with Charlie. She invited Charlie and Frankie along, so as they could discuss their findings with the Police Chief.

"Peggy has been telling me all about the new information you found." Doolan told the sparrows. "I had a look, myself, and I agree with you - I don't think Fidget is our bird. That leaves some unanswered questions, though. Who is robbing the nests? Who framed Mr Fidget? And the one I can't get my head around … Why?"

"We think we know, Mr Doolan," Charlie said. "We think it's all to do with the election. The nest robberies were carried out to make you look bad. They targeted the owls because they ultimately make the big decision. They were never going to choose you, if they were all getting robbed. Also, Johnny Fidget has been arrested three times in the past, and all by the same bird. The only one who stands to gain from all of this, and the one who arrested Fidget before, was Detective Paulie Pratchett."

"I knew it! I knew it was too good to be true. Wait a minute, though - we found evidence in Fidget's nest!"

"We think Pratchett forced Mr Finch to plant the evidence. Plus, he had his loyal sidekick helping him out: a bird by the name of Haggs."

"I know Haggs all right - how he ever got to join the police is beyond me. I can't believe all of this! We're meant to protect birds, and uphold the law, and these two are behaving like this. I'll throw both of them off the force! I'll-"

"We need to get evidence first," Peggy interrupted. "Pratchett is never going to confess of his own accord."

Just at that moment there was a knock at the door. It was the receptionist, from the front desk.

"Detective Doolan, you are very popular today. You have another visitor, there's a Mr Finch here to see you."

Detective Doolan, Peggy Beans and the two sparrows exchanged identical, flabbergasted looks.

Well, this was a turn-up for the books!

CHAPTER 26

Mr Finch speaks out

Detective Doolan, Peggy Beans and Mr Finch emerged from Doolan's office after a long meeting. All three birds looked happy with the outcome. They approached Charlie and Frankie, who were waiting patiently outside. Charlie had tried peering through the keyhole, but had been unsuccessful.

"We wouldn't normally discuss this with anyone outside of the Pigeon Police," Detective Doolan said. "However, since the two of you have been so helpful, we thought it only fair to keep you in the loop. And to ask for your help."

"You were both right about almost everything. Pratchett is the bird behind it all. He thought that, if he robbed the owls with the election coming up, it would make me look bad, and I wouldn't be re-elected. He then thought that, if he was the one who arrested the culprit, it would better his chances of getting the job."

"He wanted to be leader, very, very badly," said Peggy Beans.

"I can't believe how low he stooped to try and get the job." Doolan shook his head.

"You said that we were right about almost everything. What were we wrong about?" asked Frankie.

"It wasn't Mr Finch, on his own, breaking and entering into the owl nests." Doolan said. "Haggs and Pratchett couldn't get in the nests without smashing the doors. That's why Mr Finch was forced into helping. He's not proud of it, but he was in fear for his life. Pratchett and Haggs threatened him."

"I'm ashamed of myself," Finch said. "I've heard pupils and staff call me 'Fearsome Finchy' but the truth is, I'm not fearsome at all. I'm scared of my own shadow. I can't believe I was forced into breaking the law."

"Pratchett's a bully. There's no need to explain yourself to us," said Charlie.

"But that's it isn't it? I do need to explain. Everyone thinks I'm this terrifying teacher. Every bird in my class is frightened! I'm finished, once this gets out."

"No one will say a word about it," said Doolan.

"There's nothing at all to be ashamed of. Bullies like Pratchett exist, no matter what age, and they're the ones who should be ashamed. He'll get plenty of time to think about what he's done in prison though!"

"No-one will ever know. I'll not say a word." said Frankie.

"How's about I'll try and be less strict in class - lose the 'Fearsome Finchy' tag, once and for all?" suggested Mr Finch, hopefully.

"That would be great!" Frankie replied, happily.

"Now, that's everything just about sorted - apart from what to do with our friend, Detective Pratchett." said Peggy Beans.

Frankie and Charlie looked at each other.

"We have an idea ..."

CHAPTER 27
Caught Red Handed

"I've tracked down Finch," said Haggs.

"Excellent," said Pratchett. Good news for a change, he thought. Maybe everything wasn't going to go wrong, after all.

"No … No, it's not excellent, Paulie. He's turned up at the Police nest! And he's been talking to Doolan …

and to Peggy Beans …

and to the sparrows!"

*

Mr Finch was in his nest, sitting in his favourite chair, waiting.

It wouldn't be long before Pratchett and Haggs came to visit. He was sure of that. He knew Haggs saw him at the Police nest. He suspected the shifty bird had also followed him home.

Mr Finch wanted to be seen, though. That was the plan, after all.

Frankie and Charlie were perched in the trees across from Mr Finch's nest. Peggy Beans was with them, as were Detectives Doolan and Twittery. Frankie's friends, Geego, Kal and Spark, were also positioned in trees to the back of the nest. Charlie had also enlisted the help of Miles, in case it turned into a long chase. More Pigeon Police were perched in the surrounding trees. Mr Finch was wired up for sound, with some of the equipment Swifty the Gadget had given the sparrows.

No one would miss a thing.

They all watched as Pratchett and Haggs approached. The two pigeon's looked around. They were cautious, but not cautious enough. Haggs moved to Mr Finch's door and forced a large twig into the lock. He took too long for Pratchett. Pratchett pushed Haggs out of the way, and then put his considerable weight against the door, forcing it open. They both stumbled into the nest, and clumsily closed the door behind them.

Mr Finch couldn't fail to hear the Pigeon's enter -

"Carrington, Carrington, Carrington. Whatever are we going to do with you?" Pratchett asked. Everyone could hear clearly, through Swifty's listening device.

"What did you tell the police?" Haggs added.

"I've not spoken to the police." Finch said.

"Don't lie to us. Haggs here may look daft, but he spotted you in the Police nest."

Haggs didn't know if he was being given a compliment, or not. He smiled, in any case.

"OK, I admit it. I spoke to the police. I've told them everything." Finch said.

Haggs looked horrified, Pratchett furious.

Pratchett pulled out a large branch. He snapped it in front of Mr Finch. He held it towards Mr Finch's beak.

"I told you what would happen, if you blabbed to the police."

Mr Finch was sweating heavily. The sharp branch was far too close for comfort. *This would be a good time for the police to come in*, he thought.

"The games up Pratchett. The police know you're responsible for the nest robberies, and they know you framed Fidget. The owls know all about you, as well!" Finch said, his voice trembling a little bit.

"Why haven't I been arrested, then? You're bluffing. Voting closes in a couple of hours. I'm about to be named leader of the Pigeon Detectives. Who cares if I went about it in a different way?"

"You don't even regret anything, do you?" Mr Finch asked.

"Regret anything? Of course I don't. I'd do it all again in a heartbeat. Fidget is better off in prison. Nobody will miss him. Besides, I'm the best bird to lead the Pigeon Police. The ends justify the means!"

Detective Doolan had heard enough.

They now had a full, recorded confession.

He stormed through the nest door, with Detective Twittery.

"Detective Pratchett, I am placing you under arrest!" Detective Doolan said.

"Arrest me?!? Whatever for?" said Pratchett.

"We heard everything, Paulie. It's over."

Pratchett knew the game was up. However, he wasn't one for giving up easily. He decided to make one last, desperate, bid for freedom. Pratchett pushed Detective Doolan. He made his way towards the exit. He was past everyone and heading for the door. He was close to escaping!

Frankie flew into action. He grabbed the branch Pratchett had threatened Finch with. He managed to hook it on Pratchett's talons. He yanked it backwards, tripping the want away pigeon, exactly as he had done to Mr Fidget some time before. Pratchett spun out of control. He collided with the door of Mr Finch's nest with a loud crash. Part of the ceiling fell down onto his head.

Pratchett lay on the floor, holding his sore head and cursing everyone.

Everything was ruined, and all because of Finch and these blasted sparrows!

CHAPTER 28
All's well that ends well

Peggy Beans stood to make the election announcement. She was smiling, from ear to ear. Sat in the front row of the Owl Parliament were the two remaining candidates: Detectives Doolan and Twittery. Beside them, there was an empty seat. It had been reserved for Detective Pratchett. He wouldn't need it now.

"It is with great pleasure that I can announce that the new Pigeon Detective leader is … the one and only … Detective Doolan!"

*

"I would like to personally apologise to you, Mr Fidget." Detective Doolan said. "I can't believe how badly you have been treated. I know that no apology from me is going to make things better. You don't know how sorry we all are. I know this doesn't make up for it, but we have a little surprise for you."

Detective Doolan had got in touch with Harry Sparrow, through Charlie and Frankie. Together, they worked hard, through the night, to refurbish Mr Fidget's nest. It was completely transformed. Everything was fixed and replaced. It was now a lovely little nest.

"Oh, my goodness! My nest! It's fit for a king!"

Johnny Fidget leapt up into the air. He was delighted.

"I can't thank you all enough."

*

Charlie Sparrow nailed his new sign onto the office door.

'Charlie and Frankie Sparrow: Private Investigators.'

Things couldn't have worked out any better for Charlie and Frankie Sparrow. They had saved Johnny Fidget from spending a long time in jail for crime's he didn't commit, they had saved Mr Finch from

Pratchett's clutches, and they had saved Detective Doolan's job.

Things had worked out brilliantly.

If Pratchett's plan had worked, he would be Pigeon Detective leader instead of Doolan. Instead, he was to be thrown off the Police force and into jail, along with his partner in crime, Haggs.

The two sparrows had not only solved the case of the missing schoolteacher, they had caught the nest robber as well.

Two, for the price of one!

One thing was for sure, this wouldn't be the last case Charlie would solve, and it would all be with a little bit of help from his young nephew, Frankie Sparrow.

THE END

FREE STUFF!

Sign up for loads of free stuff! No catch. You'll receive:
an occasional Frankie Sparrow newsletter,
Uncle Charlie Sparrow's confidential case files
and lots of other exclusive content.

All for nothing … it's free!

Sign up at: www.booksbyewan.com

Acknowledgements

Firstly, thank you for buying my book. It really is much appreciated and I hope you enjoyed it. If you didn't, I'm sorry but there will be no refunds!

I'd like to thank a few people who have helped me in writing this book and helped me in life in general. I have dedicated the book to my wife, Tricia, and son, Aaron, as they are the most special people in my life. Life is never dull with them around and I love them loads (getting a bit mushy this!) I'd like to also thank my Mum and Dad who are always there for me and I'd like to thank my brothers, Gavin and Ross. Thank you to my lovely in-laws, Sheila, who read the book at an early stage and Big Toe George.

Thanks to all at Polgarus Studio's and especially Kate Gordon who did a cracking job with editing. Many thanks also to the lovely folks at SP101 - Mark Dawson, James Blatch and the team have been inspirational. Thank you also to Stuart Bache for the wonderful cover.

Writing a book was always a dream of mine. Don't let anyone tell you, you can't do something!

Thanks again.

You can contact Ewan by going to his website at: www.booksbyewan.com or follow him on Twitter, @EwanMcGregor187.